THE
UNOFFICIAL
JOKE BOOK
FOR FANS OF
Harry Potter

ALSO BY BRIAN BOONE:

Hysterical Jokes for Minecrafters:
Blocks, Boxes, Blasts, and Blow-Outs, Book 3

Side-Splitting Jokes for Minecrafters:
Ghastly Golems and Ghoulish Ghasts, Book 4

Jokes for Minecrafters: Uproarious Riddles for Minecrafters:
Mobs, Ghasts, Biomes, and More! Book 5

Jokes for Minecrafters: Gut-Busting Puns for Minecrafters:
Endermen, Explosions, Withers, and More! Book 6

Minecraft Know-it-All Trivia Book

THE UNOFFICIAL JOKE BOOK FOR FANS OF HARRY POTTER

VOL. 2

BRIAN BOONE

ILLUSTRATIONS BY

AMANDA BRACK

Sky Pony Press
New York

Copyright © 2018 by Hollan Publishing, Inc.

Sky Pony Press books may be purchased in bulk at special discounts for sales promotion, corporate gifts, fund-raising, or educational purposes. Special editions can also be created to specifications. For details, contact the Special Sales Department, Sky Pony Press, 307 West 36th Street, 11th Floor, New York, NY 10018 or info@skyhorsepublishing.com.

Sky Pony® is a registered trademark of Skyhorse Publishing, Inc.®, a Delaware corporation.

Visit our website at www.skyponypress.com.

10 9 8 7 6 5

Library of Congress Cataloging-in-Publication Data is available on file.

Cover artwork by Amanda Brack and iStockphoto/Shutterstock

Box Set ISBN: 978-1-5107-4816-3
Ebook ISBN: 978-1-5107-4817-0

Printed in China

CONTENTS

Introduction

First things first: Slytherins aren't all evil. Most of the witches and wizards whom the wise and wondrous Sorting Hat placed in the house founded by Salazar Slytherin embody characteristics like ambition, leadership, and drive. What's wrong with those things?

Okay, sure, it's where Tom Riddle, a.k.a. Lord Voldemort, spent his time at Hogwarts, not to mention pretty much all the Death Eaters and their kids. But it's also where some of most interesting people in the magical world received their education, such as the conflicted and complicated Snape, and good ol' Draco Malfoy. Sometimes, a Slytherin is just going to be *misunderstood.*

One more thing you might not have known about Slytherins: They love to joke, and they love to laugh. And you hold in your hands the collection just for Slytherins, future Slytherins, and Slytherin wannabes: *The Unofficial Harry Potter Joke Book for Fans of Harry Potter: Vol. 2.* In here, you'll find all sorts of jokes a Slytherin would love—jokes about spells, jokes about magical objects, jokes about magical history, and, of course, jokes about Hogwarts professors, as well as jokes about Potter and his irksome friends, Granger and Weasley.

If you *expecto* jokes, you've come to the right place. Now *lumos* the humor part of your brain . . . and your funny bone, too!

Chapter 1

LIVING THAT SLYTHERIN LIFE

Q. What's green and silver and blue?

A. A cold Slytherin.

Q. Which Canadian rapper do Slytherins like best?

A. Drake-O.

Q. What singer is the most "Royal" to Slytherins?
A. Lorde Voldemort.

•

Q. What is Draco's favorite flower?
A. The narcissus.

•

Q. What does Draco do with his leftovers?
A. He wraps them up in Mal-foil.

•

Q. What does Draco eat for breakfast?
A. Dracon and eggs.

•

Q. What cologne does Draco wear?
A. Draco Noir.

•

Q. How does Draco grab a napkin?
A. "Expecto patronapkin!"

Living That Slytherin Life

Crabbe walks into a restaurant. The waiter says, "Hey, we have a menu item named after you!" Crabbe says, "You have something called Vincent?"

•

Q. Why does Voldemort love Nagini?
A. Because she gives him lots of hisses.

•

Q. What dance do Slytherins do at the Yule Ball?
A. The Mamba.

•

Q. Did you hear they opened a Slytherins-only magic school in the US?
A. Yep, it's in Hississippi.

•

Q. Why don't Slytherins need to "solemnly swear they're up to no good"?
A. Because they always are.

Q. How do two Slytherins show they like each other?
A. They give each other a little hiss.

Slytherins aren't tattle-tales ... they're rattletails.

•

Even if you defeat Voldemort's minions, they'll still come Slytherin back.

•

Q. When is a Slytherin most unbearable?
A. When he's throwing a hissssy fit.

Living That Slytherin Life

Q. What kind of stories do Voldemort's minions tell?
A. Worm-tales.

●

Q. What do you get Voldemort for his birthday?
A. A bouquet of followers.

●

Q. What's a Slytherin's favorite class?
A. Hissssssstory.

●

Did you know that Crabbe and Goyle once thought Hogwarts
was a school at sea? They heard it was a boarding school.

●

Q. What does a Slytherin have for a light lunch?
A. A sssssssalad.

●

Q. What should you always do at Malfoy Manor?
A. Mind your Malfoy manners!

Q. Did you hear that Professor Snape gave Draco an A+?
A. His project on *expelliarmus* knocked him over!

•

Q. What was Voldemort's parents' favorite game?
A. "Got your nose!"

•

Q. What can you do that Voldemort can't?
A. Sneeze—he has no nose!

•

Q. When do Slytherins eat cake?
A. When it's time for desssssssssert.

•

Q. How do you make a Slytherin stew?
A. Keep them waiting for a few hours.

•

Q. What's silver and green and silver and green?
A. A Slytherin rolling down a hill.

Q. What's Snape's favorite flower?
A. Lilies.

●

Q. Why do they call him the Bloody Baron?
A. Because the Not-So-Bloody-Baron would be a mouthful.

●

Q. What kind of horn will you never hear in the Hogwarts band?
A. A Slughorn.

●

Q. Why did Voldemort never know when his kettle was boiling?
A. Because the "T" is silent.

●

Q. What's a Slytherin's favorite fast-food place?
A. Draco Bell.

Q. What's the hottest place on Earth for a Slytherin?
A. The desssssssert.

Q. When is purple not really purple?
A. When it's Lavender … Brown.

Q. Do worms have tails?
A. Sure, if they're Wormtails.

Living That Slytherin Life

Q. What's a Slytherin's favorite vegetable?
A. Asp-aragus.

•

Q. What does Bellatrix take for an upset stomach?
A. Aunt-acid.

•

Q. Did you hear that Bellatrix lived to be very old?
A. She was an aunt-tique.

•

Q. How does Bellatrix take her pizza?
A. With aunt-chovies.

•

Q. What comedy do Slytherins like best?
A. Monty Python.

•

Q. Why doesn't Voldemort like baseball?
A. Because you only get three strikes.

Q. What do Slytherins call Voldemort?

A. Hissssss Majesty.

•

Q. Did you hear about the Slytherin beauty queen?

A. She won Hisssss America!

Q. Did you hear Voldemort broke his leg?

A. He had to walk around on horcrutches.

10

Q. What's the difference between a Slytherin and a Gryffindor?

A. Gryffindors do dumb and dangerous things because they're dumb. Slytherins do dumb and dangerous things just because.

•

If Snape had married Lily, he would have been Not-So-Severus Snape.

•

Q. What do the zoo and Slytherin have in common?

A. They're both big on snake houses.

•

Q. Did you know that Draco is half centaur?

A. The top half!

•

Q. Why is herbology a Slytherin's favorite subject?

A. Because it's held in the green house.

11

Q. What kind of apples do Slytherins like best?

A. Crabbe apples.

●

Q. What do a rubber knife and the House Cup standings have in common?

A. The points are meaningless!

●

Q. What's the worst part about being a teenage Death Eater?

A. You get zits *and* a Dark Mark.

●

Q. What's Draco's aunt's favorite show?

A. *LeStranger Things*.

●

Doctor: What is your blood type?
Draco: PURE!

Q. What's a Slytherin's favorite Christmas carol?

A. "Green and Silver Bells".

•

Q. What happens when you mix potato chips with pieces of Voldemort's soul?

A. Horcrunches.

Q. Do Slytherins celebrate Earth Day?

A. No. They've been "green" for centuries!

•

Q. Professor: Where do you see yourself in five years?

A. Slytherin Student: Azkaban.

•

Q. What's self-assured, blunt, and sleeps in a tree for twenty hours a day?

A. A Slotherin.

14

Living That Slytherin Life

Q. What can you break in Slytherin and not get in trouble?

A. The rules.

●

Q. What did the Slytherin waiting for a light at the end of the tunnel do?

A. Lit the light.

●

Q. Did you hear that Slytherin broke up with her boyfriend?

A. She said, "It's not me. It's you."

●

Q. How do Slytherins take their chocolate?

A. Dark and bitter.

●

Have you ever seen the giant squid pass by the Slytherin common room? You haven't? It's ink-credible!

Q. Why don't Slytherins ever pick a fight with the squid that passes by their common room?

A. It's well-armed.

•

Q. What do Slytherins drink out of?

A. House Cups.

Q. What's the one thing colder than a Dementor's kiss?

A. The Slytherin common room.

•

Voldemort's mother went to the beach to get a tan, but she still came back looking quite Gaunt.

Q. Why was Pansy Parkinson given a position of power?

A. Because she was Little Miss Prefect!

●

Q. What does Pansy Parkinson wear to class?

A. Pansy's pants.

●

Q. Why didn't Harry Potter wind up with the Sorting Hat's first choice?

A. He slythered his way out of it.

Remember, nobody's prefect—except for Tom Riddle,
Lucius Malfoy, Draco, Pansy Parkinson …

•

Q. Did you hear that Draco cast some magic on Potter?
A. He was out for a spell.

•

**Q. What do you get when you cross a sea animal with
Voldemort's daughter?**
A. Dolphoni.

•

Q. How does Draco enter a room?
A. He slithers in.

•

Q. How do you confuse a Slytherin?
A. You tell them a Tom Riddle.

Living That Slytherin Life

Q. What's a Slytherin's favorite movie?

A. *Snakes on a Plane.*

●

Q. What's a Slytherin's *other* favorite movie?

A. *Snapes on a Plane.*

●

Q. Why couldn't Nearly Headless Nick be head of house for Slytherin?

A. Because he was headless.

●

Q. Why else couldn't Nearly Headless Nick be head of house for Slytherin?

A. Because he was a Gryffindor.

●

Q. Why did the vampire want to be admitted to Slytherin?

A. He heard there was nothing but pure blood there.

Q. What kind of horns does a Slytherin have?

A. Slughorns.

Q. Why are Slytherins so good at keeping secrets?

A. Because they have a whole Chamber in which to store them!

•

Q. What should you do if you find Salazar Slytherin's favorite talisman?

A. Locket!

Chapter 2

DRACO'S BURN WARD

Ron: It took three sheep to make this sweater.
Draco: I didn't know they could knit!

●

Ron: I spent eight hours on my homework last night.
Draco: Did it fall under the bed?
Ron: …yes.

●

Q. What's the sharpest house in Hogwarts?
A. Gryffindor, because Dumbledore is always giving them points.

●

Q. What's the greatest April Fool's Day prank ever played on the world?
A. Fred and George Weasley's birthday.

Q. What's the house animal of Gryffindor?

A. The porcupine. They have a ton of points for no reason!

Q. What's the difference between Slytherins and Gryffindors?

A. Slytherins are serpents, and Gryffindors should be servants.

•

Q. Why wouldn't Draco visit Pottermore?

A. Because why would he want more Potter?

Draco's Burn Ward

Q. Did you hear about Draco's baking accident?
A. He put so much ginger in a ginger cake that he called it a Weasley.

●

Q. Why did they call it the Triwizard Tournament?
A. Because when Harry was in it, he really had to try hard.

●

Harry Potter walked into a bar. Because they were on his windows.

●

Why do they call them points if there's no point to them? Gryffindor is just going to get House Cup anyway!

●

Q. What does Harry Potter say literally all the time?
A. "Shut up, Draco!"

●

Q. What do you call an idiot who wears glasses?
A. Harry Potter.

23

Q. What do you call that useless piece of flesh surrounding a scar?

A. Harry Potter.

•

Q. Why did Parvati Patil have a bad time at the Yule Ball?

A. Because Harry brought her.

•

Q. How many Harry Potters does it take to screw in a light bulb?

A. Only the one. He just stands there, and the world revolves around him.

•

Q. Why does Neville have to use two bathroom stalls?

A. Because he has a longbottom.

•

Q. What should Harry use his quidditch broomstick for?

A. Cleaning!

24

Draco's Burn Ward

Q. Why did the Sorting Hat place Crabbe and Goyle in Slytherin?

A. It figured it was easier for them to spell than "Hufflepuff."

•

Q. What outfit looks best on a Gryffindor?

A. An invisibility cloak.

25

Q. Why does Crabbe always stand on the left and Goyle on the right?

A. So Draco can tell them apart.

●

Q. Want to hear a joke from a Slytherin?

A. Hufflepuff.

●

Q. Want to hear another one?

A. Harry Potter.

Q. What do you call a Hufflepuff with two brain cells?

A. Blessed.

●

Q. Why did Crabbe and Goyle cross the road?

A. Because Draco did.

●

You're so Muggle, you thought the Floo Network was on channel 44.

Q. How does a Slytherin run?

A. In a serpentine fashion.

Hagrid is so hairy that he makes a bowling ball look fuzzy.

•

Q. How many Hufflepuffs does it take to screw in a lightbulb?

A. All of them.

•

Q. Why did the Weasley cross the road?

A. Somebody tossed a knut out there.

Q. How could Potter even attend Hogwarts?

A. He got a "fool" scholarship.

●

Q. Did you hear about the Hufflepuff who didn't want to win the end-of-the-year points contest?

A. She thought it was gross that the whole house would have to share one cup!

●

Q. What's the most unrealistic thing at Hogwarts?

A. That Ron Weasley has two friends.

●

Q. What do you call someone who's a wizard and somehow doesn't realize it for 11 years?

A. Harry Potter.

●

It's funny how Harry Potter is supposedly such a great seeker, but he couldn't capture *one* out of thousands of Hogwarts letters swirling all around him.

If Draco wrote the Harry Potter Books
- *Harry Potter and the Sorcerer's Groan*
- *Harry Potter and Shame-Ber of Secrets*
- *Harry Potter Should Be a Prisoner of Azkaban*
- *Harry Potter and the Goblet of Fire He Used to Cheat*
- *Harry Potter and the Mudblood Prince*
- *Harry Potter and the Order of the Phoenix is No Match*
- *Harry Potter is Deathly Annoying*

•

Q. Did you hear that Neville ate his wand after a *lumos* spell?

A. He wanted a light snack.

•

When he grows up, Harry is going to work at the Ministry of Tragic.

•

Q. Why didn't Voldemort wear glasses?

A. Because he didn't have a nose to rest them on.

Q. How do you know if a wizard is a Pure Blood?

A. They'll tell you right away.

●

Q. Why did Harry mess up the Floo Network the first time he used it?

A. He was green.

●

Q. What did the dumb wizard do when he put his name in the Goblet of Fire?

A. He blew on it because it was too hot.

Draco's Burn Ward

Wizard prank: Turn every one of someone's possessions into a Portkey.

•

Potter has such bad breath, a Dementor wouldn't even kiss him.

•

Potter is so dumb, his patronus is an empty bucket.

•

Potter is so lame that Voldemort calls *him* you-know-who.

•

Potter is so ugly, his boggart turns into a mirror.

•

Potter is so ugly, the Ministry of Magic thought he was an unregistered Animagus.

•

Potter is so lame that he doesn't show up on the Marauder's Map.

Potter's feet are so gross that house elves turn down his socks.

•

Death Eater: Potter is so lame that when a Dementor kissed me, I just had to relive the times I've talked to him.

•

Q. How does George Weasley eat corn?
A. By the ear.

•

Draco walked into Dumbledore's office. "Ten points from Slytherin," Dumbledore said.

•

Q. Who's the only Potter a Slytherin might like?
A. Beatrix Potter.

•

Q. What's a Slytherin's favorite rock band?
A. Silver and Green Day.

Draco's Burn Ward

Q. What show does Draco assume is about Harry?
A. *You're the Worst.*

•

Q. Why does Ron think spells are called that?
A. Because their names are so hard to spell!

•

Potter is so pale, he makes Moaning Myrtle look sunburned.

•

Did you hear about the dumb wizard who shoved a package in his mouth? He wanted to be a Parseltongue.

Hufflepuff student: Can I ask a dumb question?
Slytherin student: I wouldn't expect anything less.

•

Q. Why did the Hufflepuff return his house tie?
A. It was too tight.

Q. How can you tell if you're a Hufflepuff?
A. You're barely mentioned in the Harry Potter books.

Draco's Burn Ward

To Ron Weasley, *every* book is a mystery.

●

Q. What can you always count on in a Snape class?
A. *Expecto moboredom*!

●

Q. How do you find Dumbledore in a crowd?
A. Say "Slytherin won the House Cup" and he'll show up and give it to Gryffindor instead.

●

Q. Did you hear the joke about Harry Potter?
A. It stinks.

●

Harry: I heard what you said about me, Draco.
Draco: Good!

Chapter 3

AROUND HOGWARTS

Q. How did Nearly Headless Nick tell Peeves it was safe to roam Hogwarts?

A. "The ghost is clear!"

●

Q. How are young wizards like fish?

A. They're in a school.

Q. Why was Nearly Headless Nick jealous of Dumbledore?

A. Because after supper in the Great Hall, *he* wanted to be the after-dinner spooker.

●

Did you hear Hogwarts let Nearly Headless Nick teach a class? He went through his lesson on walking through walls over and over again.

●

Q. What's the difference between Potter and Hagrid?

A. One's a wizard named Harry, the other is a hairy wizard.

●

Q. Who does Professor Snape always blame when something goes wrong?

A. His Snape goat.

●

Q. How does Professor Snape avoid trouble?

A. He takes the e-Snape route.

Q. What do you get when you cross Sirius Black with Remus Lupin?

A. Daring puppies.

●

Q. What's Professor Lupin's favorite holiday?

A. Howl-o-ween.

Q. How do you cross from the Slytherin bunks into Hogwarts?

A. You take the um-bridge.

Q. Why did Snape deduct points from the classroom clock?

A. Because it kept ticking.

•

Q. What's the difference between the Hogwarts Express conductor and a Hogwarts professor?

A. One minds the train and the other trains the mind.

•

Q. What kind of math class do they teach at Hogwarts?

A. Arithmatricks!

•

Q. Do they have gym class at Hogwarts?

A. No, but they do exorcise.

•

Q. Did you hear that Ron Weasley went to Madame Pomfrey?

A. He was sick of doing homework!

Q. Did you know Mrs. Norris works at Hogwarts?
A. Yes, she does a little mousework.

Q. Why is Hermione so good at catching fish?
A. Because she's a bookworm.

•

Q. Mad-Eye Moody must be a good teacher.
A. He has lots of pupils.

•

Q. Why are there never any class trips at Hogwarts?
A. Because all the kids stayed upright.

Around Hogwarts

Q. Did you hear Filch got to do some gardening around Hogwarts?

A. He planted cattails, of course.

•

Q. Why did Professor Snape jump in the lake?

A. He wanted to test the water.

•

Q. Where did Harry take Cho Chang?

A. To a history class — it was full of dates.

•

Hermione: Ron, you missed class yesterday.
Ron: I wouldn't say I missed it.

•

Q. Why did Hermione take a sponge to her Defense Against the Dark Arts class?

A. Because it was very absorbing.

41

Hogwarts has lots of school spirit. There's Peeves, Nearly
Headless Nick, Moaning Myrtle …

•

Q. What's a good homework resource for student wizards?
A. Witch-a-pedia.

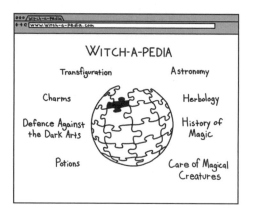

Ron: Did you find the test questions easy?
Harry: Sure, but the answers were hard.

•

Oddly enough, the one class they never taught at Hogwarts
was pottery.

Q. What did the Fat Lady want to do with her day?
A. Just hang around.

•

Q. What kind of jokes does Madame Pomfrey tell?
A. Sick ones.

•

Q. Did you hear that Lupin swallowed a clock?
A. He got ticks.

•

Student: Madame Pomfrey, help! My dad turned into a dog!
Madame Pomfrey: Is it Sirius?

•

Did you hear that Harry Potter had a crush on a classmate?
   He's the boy who loved!

•

Q. What puzzle game infuriates Hagrid?
A. A Rubeus Cube.

Q. How do not-very-smart cows get into Hogwarts?
A. Through the dumb-bull-door.

**Q. Did you hear that Viktor skipped a Triwizard
    Tournament task?**
A. He just felt too krummy.

•

Did you hear that Viktor was so hungry after the Triwizard
    Tournament that he ate all the food in the Great Hall?
    There was nothing left but krums.

Around Hogwarts

Q. Did you hear that Hogwarts gets foreign aid?

A. Yep, Krum brought a tutor when he came.

•

It Just Doesn't Make Sense

- If Harry Potter is so great, how come he doesn't make a spell to make it so he doesn't need glasses?
- Why didn't they use the Time Turner to save, like, everything?
- It must be awkward how Ron is still in love with Fleur, who is married to his brother.
- Harry goes into Honeydukes while invisible and takes … a lollipop from his friend? That's not very nice!

•

Q. What kind of wells would you find on the Hogwarts grounds?

A. Inkwells.

•

Q. What are Luna's favorite thing to watch?

A. *Luna Tunes.*

45

Q. What should tests at Hogwarts be called?

A. Quizards.

•

Q. Do they teach science at Hogwarts?

A. Sure, in the labracadabra.

Q. Did you know that Dumbledore was a brain surgeon?

A. Yep, he was a real head master.

Q. Which professor loves roller coasters?

A. Remus Loop-de-Lupin.

•

Q. Who does Lupin transform into at Christmas?

A. Santa Claws.

•

Q. What do you get if you cross the author of Harry Potter and Professor Lupin?

A. J.K. Howling.

•

Q. Can a broomstick fly higher than the highest tower of Hogwarts?

A. Of course. Hogwarts can't fly!

•

Harry: I fell off my broomstick and bonked my head.
Oliver: Did you see Madame Pomfrey?
Harry: No, just stars.

Q. What keeps the lake around Hogwarts full?

A. The headmaster has a re-moat control.

•

Q. What do Hagrid and a keychain have in common?

A. They're both a keeper of keys.

Q. Did you hear Hermione changed her name to sound tough?

A. Call her Hermione Danger now.

Q. What do you get when you cross a pink-haired auror with a war machine?

A. Nymphadora Tanks.

●

Q. Why was Professor Quirrell a terrible soccer player?

A. He hated taking headers.

●

Q. If Dumbledore was a basketball player, what position would he play?

A. Point guard.

Chapter 4:

Q. What do you get when you cross a Portkey with Skele-Gro?

A. A skeleton key.

Q. What's the first spell wizard babies learn?

A. A cribbing spell.

50

Spells, Potions, and Magical Objects

A wizard walks into the Leaky Cauldron and orders a
  Forgetfulness Potion. He turns to the wizard next to him
  and says, "So, do I come here often?"

•

Tom says, "We don't serve time travelers here."
Hermione walks into the Leaky Cauldron with a Time Turner.

•

Q. What spell could whisk you off to Hawaii?
A. *Aloha-mora!*

Q. How does a wizard put on a pair of jeans?

A. *Levis-osa!*

Q. Do kids ever get kicked out of Hogwarts?

A. No, they get expelliarmused.

•

Q. Did you hear that Voldemort used a lightning spell?

A. It was quite shocking.

•

Q. Why couldn't Harry bust through platform 9 3/4?

A. He hadn't been properly trained.

Did you know there's a holiday celebrating Ireland's contributions to wizarding? It's called St. Patronus Day.

●

Q. How do wizards send a package?

A. *Federo Expecto!*

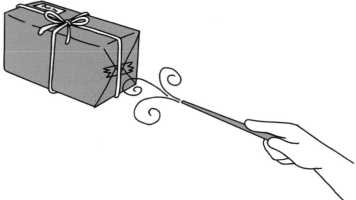

Q. Did you hear about the kids who were swearing in Hogwarts?

A. They were using the Marauder's Map.

●

Q. How do you chop magical firewood?

A. With an Accio.

Q. How do you ask a magical question?
A. Just Accio.

•

Q. What spell would you use to make mushrooms appear?
A. A confungus charm.

Q. Did you hear about the wizard who disappeared in the bathroom?
A. He went to powder his nose and accidentally used Floo Powder.

Spells, Potions, and Magical Objects

Q. How does a wizard unlock their phone?

A. *Alohomora!*

•

Q. What does a wizard keep in their sleeves?

A. Their expelliarms.

•

Q. How did the dumb wizard try to get a dog?

A. *Expecto pet-ronum!*

•

Q. How do you make Mrs. Norris meow?

A. A caterwauling charm.

•

Poor Voldemort. He was hit with an impenetrable *Calvario* curse.

•

Q. Did you hear what happened to the wizard with a *Calvario* curse?

A. Hair today, gone tomorrow.

Q. What's the worst spell to use to make breakfast?
A. The cornflake skin spell.

•

Q. What kind of kiss does Harry Potter not want?
A. A Dementor's kiss.

•

Q. What did Ron say after Hermione cast a *lumos* spell?
A. "You glow, girl!"

•

Q. In what part of the school day do wizards learn the *lumos* spell?
A. During Glow-and-Tell.

•

Q. How do wizards get to Las Vegas?
A. *Avada Nevada!*

•

Q. What do wizards drink on Christmas?
A. Jollyjuice potion.

Q. How do wizards make an omelet?

A. *Egg-spelliarmus!*

Harry can speak to snakes, but did you know that Professor Sprout could talk to herbs? Yep, she spoke parsleytongue.

•

Q. What happened when Professor Sprout got a hold of Hermione's magical object?

A. She turned it into a Thyme Turner.

Hermione got way too into her Time Turner, but that's all in the past now.

•

Q. Can wands interact with one another?
A. Cores they can.

•

Q. How do you know that's what you *really* desire?
A. Because Erised so.

•

Q. What's the one weed you wouldn't mind growing in your yard?
A. Gillyweed.

•

Q. What spell do you use to make citrus fruit glow?
A. *Lemos!*

•

Hogwarts is the only place where a cast comes before an injury.

Chapter 5:

Knock-knock.
Who's there?
Blue.
Blue who?
Blue up your Potions assignment
   again?

Knock-knock.
Who's there?
Oliver Wood.
Oliver Wood who?
Oliver Wood what?

•

Knock-Knock.
Who's there?
Jason.
Jason who?
Jason is what chasers do in quidditch.

•

Knock-knock.
Who's there?
Althea.
Althea who?
Althea in the Room of Requirement for DA training!

Knock-Knockturn Alley

Knock-knock.
Who's there.
Gwen.
Gwen who?
Gwen the Room of Requirement and stay there!

●

Knock-knock.
Who's there?
Sawyer.
Sawyer who?
Sawyer picture in *The Daily Prophet.*

●

Knock-Knock.
Who's there?
Butternut.
Butternut who?
Butternut go into the Forbidden Forest!

Knock-knock.
Who's there?
Hufflepuff.
Hufflepuff who?
I'll Hufflepuff and blow your house down!

•

Knock-knock.
Who's there?
Alma.
Alma who?
Alma new magic textbooks
   are so heavy!

Knock-Knockturn Alley

Knock-knock.
Who's there?
Micah.
Micah who?
Micah spell and save us!

Knock-knock!
Who's there?
Orange.
Orange who?
Orange you glad you didn't get sorted into Hufflepuff?

Knock-knock!
Who's there?
Maya.
Maya who?
Maya hand is killing me after Professor Umbridge's
     punishment.

Knock-knock!

Who's there?

Ralph.

Ralph who?

Ralph! Ralph! Ralph! It's me, Fluffy!

●

Knock-knock!

Who's there?

Al.

Al who?

Al give you a chocolate frog if you let me in!

Knock-Knockturn Alley

Knock-knock!
Who's there?
Mara.
Mara who?
Mara of Erised will reveal all!

Knock-knock!
Who's there?
Anita.
Anita who?
Anita new broomstick after that quidditch match!

●

Knock-knock!
Who's there?
Bree.
Bree who?
Bree a good wizard and join the DA!

●

Knock-knock!
Who's there?
Hugh.
Hugh who?
Hugh know who!

Knock-Knockturn Alley

Knock-knock!
Who's there?
Fred.
Fred who?
Fred and George Weasley!

●

Knock-knock!
Who's there?
Mikey.
Mikey who?
Mikey didn't take me to the Quidditch World Cup!

●

Knock-knock!
Who's there?
Siri.
Siri who?
Siri you got sorted into the wrong house!

Knock-knock!
Who's there?
Nona.
Nona who?
Nona your business, MUGGLE!

●

Knock-knock!
Who's there?
Hannah.
Hannah who?
Hannah me a chocolate frog!

●

Knock-knock!
Who's there?
Wendy.
Wendy who?
Wendy last time Voldemort was this powerful?

Knock-Knockturn Alley

Knock-knock!
Who's there?
Freighter.
Freighter who?
Freighter Voldemort? Of course!

•

Knock-knock!
Who's there?
Frida.
Frida who?
Frida spiders,
    are you?

Knock-knock!
Who's there?
Mister.
Mister who?
Mister train to Hogwarts!

Knock-knock!
Who's there?
Uriah.
Uriah who?
Keep Uriah the
    snitch!

Knock-Knockturn Alley

Knock-knock!
Who's there?
Griffin.
Griffin who?
Why you Griffin me such a hard time?

●

Knock-knock!
Who's there?
Owl.
Owl who?
Owl see you later!

●

Knock-knock!
Who's there?
Daisy.
Daisy who?
Daisy plays quidditch, and at night he studies.

Knock-knock!
Who's there?
Arlette.
Arlette who?
Arlette the Chamber of Secrets open, sorry.

•

Knock-knock!
Who's there?
Celeste.
Celeste who?
Celeste time anyone saw Voldemort?

•

Knock-knock!
Who's there?
Alma.
Alma who?
Alma treasure is in Gringotts.

Knock-Knockturn Alley

Knock-knock!
Who's there?
Linda.
Linda who?
Linda hand, we can't beat Voldemort on our own.

●

Knock-knock!
Who's there?
Rita.
Rita who?
Rita book, you might learn something, Potter!

●

Knock-knock!
Who's there?
Phyllis.
Phyllis who?
Phyllis cup up with butterbeer, please!

Knock-knock!

Who's there?

Aida.

Aida who?

Aida too many sweets off the trolley and now I'm feeling
  sick!

Knock-Knockturn Alley

Knock-knock!
Who's there?
Rhona.
Rhona who?
Rhona broomstick all day playing quidditch and I'm
    exhausted.

●

Knock-knock!
Who's there?
Sabrina.
Sabrina who?
Sabrina long time since Harry's scar bothered him.

●

Knock-knock!
Who's there?
Meg.
Meg who?
Meg up your mind, Snape!

Knock-knock!
Who's there?
Dishes.
Dishes who?
Dishes dementors!

Knock-knock!
Who's there?
Dozen.
Dozen who?
Dozen anyone think Voldemort is growing stronger?

Knock-knock!
Who's there?
Saber.
Saber who?
Saber, Harry! Ginny is in the Chamber of Secrets!

Knock-Knockturn Alley

Knock-knock!
Who's there?
Abby.
Abby who?
Abby Christmas, Harry!

●

Knock-knock!
Who's there?
James.
James who?
James if anything happened to you, Potter.

●

Knock-knock!
Who's there?
Albus.
Albus who?
Albus out laughing if I see your boggart!

Knock-knock.
Who's there?
Minerva.
Minerva who?
Minerva you, sneaking around Hogwarts at night!

Knock-knock!
Who's there?
Athena.
Athena who?
Athena the past in
    the Pensieve!

Knock-Knockturn Alley

Knock-knock.
Who's there?
Severus.
Severus who?
Severus some money and buy a used wand.

•

Knock-knock.
Who's there?
Luke.
Luke who?
Don't Luke down when you're playing quidditch!

•

Knock-knock.
Who's there?
Justin.
Justin who?
You're Justin time for class, Hermione.

Knock-knock.
Who's there?
Time.
Time who?
Time to turn back time, Hermione.

●

Knock-knock.
Who's there?
Bane.
Bane who?
Bane thinks he's the centaur of the universe!

●

Knock-knock.
Who's there?
Venice.
Venice who?
Venice the Triwizard Tournament?

Knock-Knockturn Alley

Knock-knock.
Who's there?
Juno.
Juno who?
Juno what they're serving in the Great Hall tonight?

●

Knock-knock.
Who's there?
Sarah.
Sarah who?
Sarah doctor? We've got a bad quidditch injury here!

●

Knock-knock.
Who's there?
Buckbeak.
Buckbeak who?
Buckbeak good pals with Hagrid.

Knock-knock.
Who's there?
Unity.
Unity who?
Unity sweater for Harry again, Mrs. Weasley?

Knock-knock.
Who's there?
Alaska.
Alaska who?
Alaska my father to tell your father, WEASLEY.

Knock-Knockturn Alley

Knock-knock.
Who's there?
Anita.
Anita who?
Anita Room of Requirement!

●

Knock-knock.
Who's there?
Doughnut.
Doughnut who?
Doughnut open the Chamber of Secrets!

●

Knock-knock.
Who's there?
Waddle.
Waddle who?
Waddle we do when you're with the Dursleys all summer,
    Harry?

Knock-knock.
Who's there?
Snow.
Snow who?
Snow point trying magic if you're a Squib!

●

Knock-knock.
Who's there?
Hallways.
Hallways who?
Hallways have your wand ready to go!

●

Knock-knock.
Who's there?
Athena.
Athena who?
Athena Vestral!

Knock-Knockturn Alley

Knock-knock.
Who's there?
Avenue.
Avenue who?
Avenue been spying on me, Potter?

•

Knock-knock.
Who's there?
Chauffeur.
Chauffeur who?
Chauffeur, Harry hasn't figured out his Triwizard task.

•

Knock-knock.
Who's there?
Weird.
Weird who?
Weird you get that Elder Wand?

Chapter 6:

IT'S A MAGICAL WORLD

Q. Why is it hard to keep a secret in Gringotts?
A. Because of all the tellers.

•

Q. What does a photographer for *The Daily Prophet* **say when she takes a picture?**
A. "Hocus focus!"

Q. What part of *The Daily Prophet* has the financial news?
A. "The Daily Profit."

•

Q. Why did the wizard go live on a farm?
A. He wanted to see hog warts up close.

Q. Why is Voldemort a terrific bowler?
A. He always kills the spare.

•

Q. Why did Voldemort call a tow truck?
A. He killed the spare.

Q. When can Voldemort make you happy?

A. When he kills despair.

•

Q. What rapper do Hufflepuffs prefer?

A. Hufflepuff Daddy.

•

Q. What band do Potterheads like best?

A. The Rowling Stones.

•

Q. What's a wizard's favorite Beatles album?

A. *Magical Mystery Tour.*

•

Q. Did you hear about the witch who won the lottery?

A. She went completely knuts!

•

Q. What flowers are planted around Azkaban?

A. Mari-ghouls.

Q. How many wizards does it take to screw in a lightbulb?

A. Two. One to hold the bulb and one to rotate the room with magic.

●

Q. What cologne does the Dark Lord wear?

A. Vold Spice.

Q. What's the difference between a dog and a werewolf?

A. One pants and the other *wears* pants.

●

Q. What class is taught at Diagon Alley?

A. Buy-ology.

●

Q. Where do they train aurors in America?

A. In the state of Auroregon.

●

Q. What do mountain climbing and Gringotts have in common?

A. One employs grips and hooks, and the other employs Griphook.

●

8 Ways You Can Tell You're Not a Potterhead

- You think "quidditch" is a spell.
- Your favorite characters are Edward and Bella.
- You think Harry and Hermione wind up together.
- You think the Triwizard Tournament is won by Katniss.

It's A Magical World

- You call a wand a "magic twig."
- You think "Rowling" rhymes with "cow thing."
- When someone asks you in what house the Sorting Hat would place you, you say, "Narnia."
- You think the headmaster of Hogwarts is Gandalf.
- You tried to eat Cornelius Fudge.

●

Did you hear they built a magical school for Americans in the Midwest? It sits right on Lake Eerie.

●

Did you hear that each night in the Wizarding World, the sky lights up with beautiful colors? It's called the Auror Borealis.

●

Q. Do you want to hear a story about the Dursleys' house?
A. Well, it's Privet!

●

Q. What do you call a friend you meet shopping for wizard supplies?
A. A Diagon ally.

Q. How do you make a magical boat travel?
A. You need a couple of aurors.

Did you hear that Harry Potter kept getting points even after he was an adult? He bought a lot of steak knives.

•

Q. What's hollow but full of history?
A. Godric's Hollow.

•

Q. Where would you find a lot of bad wizards?
A. Hexico.

Q. What do you call a bunch of magic students walking in the snow?

A. A wizard blizzard.

Q. What's the worst kind of greeting in the wizarding world?

A. Deathly hellos.

Q. What language do mail truck drivers speak?

A. Parcel-tongue.

Q. What wizard shop has the best deals?

A. Bargain and Burkes.

Q. What wizard shop does Hermione like best?

A. Borgin and Books.

Q. What wizard bookshop is loved by automatons?
A. Flourish and Bots!

●

Q. Did you hear they opened a school just for ghosts?
A. Yep, Boo-batons Academy of Magic.

Q. What kind of parties do they have in the Forbidden Forest?
A. Lumber parties.

Q. Where did all the Hogwarts students buy clothes for the Yule Ball?

A. At the Yule Mall.

●

Q. What do you get when you cross a non-magical person born to wizards with a wizard tabloid?

A. A Squibbler.

●

Q. What crime show is popular in Azkaban?

A. *The Dementalist.*

●

Q. What's Harry Potter's favorite thing to do on a Saturday?

A. Miniature golf. JK, bowling.

Chapter 7:

Q. Why do Acromantulas spin webs?

A. Because they don't know how to knit.

•

Q. Why is Bane the centaur so clumsy?

A. Because he has two left feet.

•

Q. Where do wizards take care of sick centaurs?

A. In the horsepital.

•

Q. How many centaurs does it take to light up a single wand?

A. Two. One says the spell, the other keeps mentioning how bright the wand is.

Q. How did Firenze buy his home?

A. Through Centaury 21.

•

Q. How did the phoenix get kicked out of the zoo?

A. It was fired.

•

Q. What's the first thing a phoenix does in the morning?

A. Rise.

•

Q. What's a phoenix's favorite holiday?

A. Guy Fawkes Day.

•

Q. What kind of exercises does Fawkes do?

A. Warm-ups.

•

Q. Why wasn't Dumbledore afraid of the phoenix?

A. He had a fire extinguisher.

Creatures and Beasts

Q. Why wouldn't the snake talk to the Parseltongue speaker?

A. Well, they didn't know each other very well.

•

Q. What are Buckbeak and Hagrid to each other?

A. Beast friends forever.

•

Q. When was Hedwig always sick?

A. During flew season.

•

Q. What's Hagrid's brother's favorite kind of soda?

A. Grawp soda.

•

Q. Where does Grawp sit?

A. Wherever he likes!

•

Q. Why did baby Nagini cry?

A. She lost her rattle.

Q. Did you hear centaurs have cell phones?

A. Sure, it's the 21st centaury.

Q. How can you tell if someone is a boggart?

A. Because they look riddikulus!

•

Q. When is a post not a post?

A. When it's the Owl Post.

100

Creatures and Beasts

Q. Why are there no aardvarks at Hogwarts?
A. Because they aren't wizards.

•

Q. Where do wizard dogs go to relax?
A. Dogsmeade.

•

Did you hear about the forgetful owl? It could never remember who it was supposed to deliver to and would always ask, "Who?"

•

Q. Why could Harry always trust Hedwig?
A. Because she once told him, "Owl be there for you."

•

Q. How do you get magical honey?
A. You get a hive of Dumble-bees.

•

Q. When is a dog not a dog?
A. When it's a Fang!

Q. Did you hear that Aragog became a DJ?

A. He was just so good at spinning.

•

Q. Did you hear that Mrs. Norris went to her own Christmas dance?

A. It was called the Mewl Ball.

•

Q. What do you get when you cross Dobby and a hippie?

A. A house elf who says, "Sock it to me!"

Creatures and Beasts

Q. What do you call an arrogant boggart?
A. A braggart.

●

Q. What do you call a wet boggart?
A. A soggart.

●

Q. What do you get when you cross the Forbidden Forest with a boggart?
A. A loggart.

●

Q. What do boggarts drink at Christmas?
A. Eggnoggart.

●

Q. What do you get when you put a boggart in a toaster?
A. A boggart that eats Pop-Tarts.

●

Q. Are centaurs enemies?
A. No, some are Firenze.

103

Q. There were wizards in Ancient Egypt.
A. They wrote hippoglyphs on the walls.

•

Q. What do you call a mistaken hippogriff?
A. A hippo-glitch.

•

Q. What's the most beloved patronus?
A. Well, James Potter's was very deer.

Q. Firenze had a kid but she was hard to hear.

A. She was a little hoarse.

•

Q. Why would a porcupine be a great Hogwarts student?

A. It packed plenty of quills.

•

Q. How much does the average Hungarian Horntail weigh?

A. Just ask one—they come with scales.

105

Q. Did you hear about the dragon who wandered into Moaning Myrtle's bathroom?

A. It was a commode-o dragon.

●

Q. What happens when you cross a phoenix with a dragon?

A. Fire! So much fire.

●

Q. How does Dobby leave a room?

A. He turns the knobby.

●

Q. What's Hagrid's favorite board game?

A. *Hungry Hungry Hippogriffs*.

●

Q. What do you call a clever cave monster?

A. A droll troll.

●

Firenze was so arrogant. He thought he was the centaur of the universe!

Q. What do you call a pleasant magical beast?

A. A happygriff!

Q. Why did Ron love his pet rat so much?

A. It's the pet-he-grew up with.

•

DUMBLEDORE: I was talking with Fawkes the other day
and he just kept insulting me.

It's a shame I had to see him on a burning day.

107

Q. Did you hear that Hedwig dressed up in a suit of armor for Halloween?

A. She was a real knight owl.

Q. Why did Ron's rat get bigger?

A. Pettigrew!

Q. Did Dobby go to school to learn his job?

A. No, he was elf-taught.

Q. What kind of pictures does Dobby take?
A. Elfies.

•

Did you hear that Hagrid saw *How to Train Your Dragon*?
He called it *Dragon Keeping for Amateurs.*

•

Q. What's the best centaur sitcom on TV?
A. *Firenze.*

•

Q. What do you get when you cross Sirius Black and an Apple computer?
A. iPadfoot.

•

Q. What does Padfoot eat?
A. Padfood.

•

Q. What position did Nearly Headless Nick once hold?
A. Nearly Head Boy!

Q. What happens if you mix a Slytherin bigshot with a pony?

A. Horse Slughorn.

•

Did you hear about the Mandrakes that ran away from Hogwarts? They wanted to get back to their roots.

Q. How many wizards does it take to stun a dragon?

A. How many wizards have you got?

●

Q. Did you know that Salazar Slytherin's basilisk was royalty?

A. That's why they called it "Sir Pent!"

●

Q. Did you hear that Hedwig had a delivery for Harry Potter but he skipped it?

A. Yep, she just didn't give a hoot.

●

Q. Why did Nagini laugh so hard she started to cry?

A. She thought the joke was hisssssss-terical.

Chapter 8:

SOME RIDDIKULUS WORDPLAY

"The number of people not in class today bothers me," Professor Snape said absent-mindedly.

•

"I hate climbing this winding staircase," Draco said coyly.

•

"Give me another chocolate frog," Ron croaked.

•

"I was removed from my position at Hogwarts," Professor Trelawney said disappointedly.

•

"And that's all we're going to play tonight!" the Weird Sisters said disconcertingly.

Some Riddikulus Wordplay

"That was a terrible spell," said Draco disenchantedly.

•

"I hope this Skele-Gro works," Oliver Wood said disjointedly.

•

"You make me want to tear my hair out!" Voldemort said distressingly.

•

"Tonks, let's get married!" Lupin said engagingly.

•

"The Hogwarts Express is gone!" Ron said extraneously.

•

"I don't see Tonks and Lupin's boy," Hermione noted.

•

"My glasses are getting fogged up," Dumbledore said optimistically.

"Are we heading to Hagrid's house?" Hermione guessed.

●

"I lead Dumbledore's Army!" Harry said maliciously.

●

"I'd like to fix this muggle car," Arthur Weasley said
mechanically.

●

"We took third place in the House Cup race," Neville said
meddlingly.

●

"You boys are the worst!" Hermione mentioned.

●

"Boy, am I blue," said the Ravenclaw.

●

"I have a lot of children," said Molly Weasley overbearingly.

Some Riddikulus Wordplay

"The Hogwarts Express is late!" Draco railed.

•

"You snake!" Voldemort rattled to Nagini.

•

"I know all these spells by heart," Hermione wrote.

•

"My parents are dentists," Hermione said toothfully.

•

"You lose a House Cup sometimes," Harry said winsomely.

•

"The Hogwarts Express has never had an accident," Molly
    said recklessly.

•

"This garden needs more mulch," Professor Sprout
    repeated.

"So what if I'm overweight?" said Vernon roundly.

●

"I am too singing in tune," the Weird Sister sounded off.

●

"I temporarily grew powerful gills!" Harry said superficially.

●

"I work at Gringotts," said Griphook tellingly.

●

"I'm really tired of sleeping in the woods while we run from Voldemort," Ron said tensely.

●

"I flunked my O.W.L.s," said Harry testily.

●

"I'll be out of Azkaban in no time," said Sirius balefully.

●

"I want to go to the big Christmas dance," Parvati bawled.

Some Riddikulus Wordplay

"I have no idea how to answer this question," said Ron thoughtlessly.

•

"I am not full of hot air!" Aunt Marge belched.

•

"Some of these beasts need to be kept in cages," said Newt Scamander cagily.

•

"Gryffindor's quidditch team is the best," said Professor McGonagall cheerfully.

•

"My family has a great future," said Draco clandestinely.

•

"I'm ready for school to start up again," said Hermione with class.

•

"That spell threw me up into the air!" said Ginny, visibly moved.

"This is a toilet sea," Moaning Myrtle went on.

•

"We'll leave all our money to Harry," said James Potter willingly.

•

"You didn't look after my plants while I was gone?" asked Professor Sprout witheringly.

•

"Stop that centaur!" cried Dumbledore woefully.

•

"Quidditch practice is tough," Draco worked out.

•

"We're taking over now," the Death Eater cooed.

•

"Mom, Dad, I have to hypnotize you," said Hermione transparently.

Some Riddikulus Wordplay

"Gringotts doesn't want me as a depositor," said Hagrid unaccountably.

•

"I ripped my dress robes!" was Ginny's unseemly comment.

•

"I can't get a permission slip to go to Hogsmeade," said Harry unwaveringly.

•

"I can't control this flying car!" Ron maintained unswervingly.

•

"I'm meeting with some Merpeople tonight," said Dumbledore sedately.

•

"Let's go to the Forbidden Forest," Hermione ventured.

•

"This boat taking us to Hogwarts is leaking," said Hermione balefully.

Weird and Wacky Anagrams

- Draco Malfoy = "Of a cold army"
- Draco Malfoy = "Cod fly aroma"
- Harry Potter = "Threat or pry"
- Hermione Granger = "No meager herring"
- Ron Weasley = "Yes, earn owls"
- Slytherin = "Hi, sternly"
- Severus Snape = "Save pureness"
- Albus Dumbledore = "Duel durable mobs"
- Hogwarts = "Ghost war"
- Azkaban Prison = "Zap akin barons!"
- Ravenclaw = "Naval crew"
- Rubeus Hagrid = "Brash guider"
- Dolores Umbridge = "Sludgier boredom"
- Fleur Delacour = "Louder? Careful"
- Dean Thomas = "Man, so hated"
- Harry Potter = "Try hero part"
- Ollivander = "An evil lord"
- Peter Pettigrew = "Tip: a pet we regret"
- Sirius Black = "Basilisk cur"
- Platform nine and three-quarters = "Frequent trains ran to help dream"
- *Harry Potter and the Sorcerer's Stone* = "Treachery rests on transported hero"

Some Riddikulus Wordplay

- *Harry Potter and the Order of the Phoenix* = "Portrayed orphaned hero for the next hit"
- Petunia Dursley = "Easily upturned"
- Neville Longbottom = "Let not mob live long"
- Wormtail = "I'm low rat"
- Luna Lovegood = "Vague old loon"
- Rubeus Hagrid = "Bushier guard"

It's Opposite Day at Hogwarts!

- Harry Digger-Upper
- Hermione Unfarmable Land-er
- Ron Honest
- Albus Smartwindow
- Joking White
- Neville Shorttop
- Sunny Hatebad
- Draco Bonfoy
- Headless Nick
- Oliver Wouldn't

Try These Terrific Tongue Twisters

- Stan Shunpike.
- Severus Snape served and severed several snakes.
- Hufflepuffs wear ruffled puffs.
- Maybe Google Minerva McGonnagall's magical goggles?
- Potter's paltry patronus? Please.

- A hurling hex hardly harms Hermione.
- Liquid Luck leaked in my lap!
- Betcha Buckbeak bucked Bathilda Bagshot, bro.
- Vile Voldemort villainized Veela.
- Hermione halfheartedly hexed her hungry, howling half-kneazle.
- Sly Salazar Slytherin slithers sideways soundlessly.
- Severus Snape is the snarky Slytherin schoolteacher? Snape spies on scary secret societies.
- Weasleys really wheedle wisely, what?
- Lavender's Liquid Luck unluckily leaked.
- If six slithering snakes slithered up to Slytherin, would sixty slippery slippers stop Slytherin simply slipping?
- Bertie Bott better not bake a batch of botched butterscotch.

•

Riddikulus Riddles

He's a star of a series
Saw King's Cross when he was dead
Placed into Gryffindor
With a scar on his head.
Harry Potter

As the books went on
This one and Ron got closer
She corrects pronunciation
So don't mis-state *leviosa.*
Hermione

●

He was in the Potter books
From the beginning to the end
He's got a sister and five brothers
Brilliant! He's Harry's best friend!
Ron Weasley

●

All the trouble Harry Potter had
On his dark one it can be blamed
He once had a puzzling name
But now he Must Not Be Named
Voldemort

This place is unbelievably vast
Kids eat in the Great Hall
And back in 1994
It hosted the Yule Ball!
Hogwarts School of Witchcraft and Wizardry

•

This is a type of dangerous game
You win if you catch the golden snitch
Players throw balls while riding on broomsticks
The answer, of course is obviously …
Quidditch

•

A true leader in the book series
His patronus was a phoenix
He was Hogwarts' best headmaster
And he'll make you cry in book number 6
Dumbledore

Some Riddikulus Wordplay

When you first come at Hogwarts
Onto your head it is placed
It will then tell you aloud
From which of four houses you will be based
The Sorting Hat

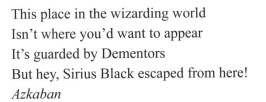

•

This place in the wizarding world
Isn't where you'd want to appear
It's guarded by Dementors
But hey, Sirius Black escaped from here!
Azkaban

•

Once the Hogwarts gamekeeper
Then promoted and he became a teacher
Half-giant, half-human
And adores all those dangerous creatures
Hagrid

He didn't like Harry Potter
The second he walked in his classroom door
Now students if you will …
Turn to page 394.
Severus Snape

●

Once thought to be a criminal
In Azkaban he was put
He was also Harry's godfather
And sometimes known as Padfoot.
Sirius Black

●

Witches and wizards but use them
So they can cast their spells as they please
It's usually made from enchantment and wood
Plus there's an Elder one of these.
Wands

Some Riddikulus Wordplay

Harry Potter ... But with Cats!

- Hairy Pawter
- Draco Mewlfoy
- Dumpurrrrrldore
- Severpuss Snape
- Hermeownie
- Ron Mewsley
- Sirius Black Cat

●

Accio ... Limericks!

The boy with a lightning-shaped scar,
Had parents who were killed by a car.
Or so his aunt said;
She put that in his head,
For her views on magic were bizarre.

●

As the quaffle flies straight to the rings,
All the Gryffindor fans start to sing:
"He'll give us the win,
And not let it in,
Because ol' Weasley is our king!"

Slytherin had a mysterious teacher,
Whose nose his most prominent feature.
He lost his true love,
And when push came to shove,
He wound up lonely and sad, just like Kreacher.

•

There once was a young pair of gingers,
At pranks, they certainly weren't beginners.
That troublesome two,
Made U-No-Poo,
At mischief they were the true winners.

•

There was once a teacher named Snape,
Who wore a black billowy cape.
When he walked through the school,
Looking tall, dark, and cool,
All the students would look at him and gape.

Some Riddikulus Wordplay

There once was a boy known by few,
He grew up and become You-Know-Who.
Also called Voldemort,
He killed muggles for sport
And everyone else he didn't like, too.

●

There once was a young orphaned boy,
Who as a child never had any toys,
But on one dark night,
Hagrid gave him a fright,
Off to Hogwarts he went filled with joy.

●

There once was a prisoner quite mad,
Who wished to get revenge on his dad.
He disguised himself as Moody,
Did Voldemort his due duty,
And Dumbledore knew he'd been had.

Hogwarts is the place to be,
Would you go if they picked ye?
Potions and spells, they'll teach you it all
And amazing supplies you can't get at the mall.
How I wish we were all able to go!

●

There was this forgetful young lad,
At Potions, he was rather quite bad.
But he proved himself brave,
Because at the end of the day
Voldemort's snakes head he had.

●

Lord Voldemort tried to kill Potter,
Who survived by the love of his mother.
A horcrux himself,
So the prophecy told,
That "one must be killed by the other."

Chapter 9:

DINNER IN THE GREAT HALL

Q. What's the difference between a mandrake and a cookie?

A. It's pretty hard to dunk a mandrake in milk.

Q. What kind of bread is served at Hogwarts?
A. Rowls.

•

Q. What's Voldemort's favorite part of a pie?
A. The Horcrux.

•

Q. What cookie do Hufflepuffs eat?
A. Fig Newt Scamanders.

•

Q. What do you get when you cross a Potions professor with the Weasleys?
A. Ginger Snapes.

•

Q. What's always served in the Ministry of Magic snack bar?
A. Cornelius Fudge.

Q. What candy do Death Eaters eat?

A. BellaTwix.

Q. Do chocolate frogs expire?

A. No, they croak.

●

Q. Why is it unpleasant to dine with Professor Lupin?

A. He just wolfs down his meals.

●

Q. What do chocolate frogs drink?

A. Croak-a-Cola.

Q. How do wizards get healthy?

A. A Polyjuice cleanse.

Q. What kind of sandwiches does Peeves eat?

A. Boo-loney.

Q. What's Ron's favorite day to go to school?

A. Sundae.

Q. What does Luna Lovegood eat for breakfast?

A. A Luna bar.

Dinner in the Great Hall

Q. Want to hear a corny joke?

A. Cornelius Fudge.

•

Q. How does the Dark Lord eat cereal?

A. Out of a Bowldemort.

•

Q. What does Nagini eat for breakfast?

A. Sssssscrambled eggs.

135

Q. What does Viktor Krum eat back home?
A. Bulger.

•

Q. Where do Neville's parents hate to eat?
A. Kentucky Petrified Chicken

•

Q. What's the most popular candy at Azkaban?
A. De-Mentos.

•

Q. How do Gryffindors measure liquid?
A. Pints!

•

Q. What would you find inside a magical roasted turkey?
A. The Giblets of Fire.

•

Q. What does Voldemort eat when he's camping?
A. A s'morecrux.

Q. What do Hufflepuffs eat for breakfast?

A. Huffle Puffs.

Q. What kind of cookies does the Hogwarts Potion master make?

A. Severus's Snaps.

•

Q. What does the Hogwarts headmaster's stomach do when it's hungry?

A. Rumbledore.

Q. What kind of seafood do Slytherins like?

A. Crabbe.

Q. What happens when you enchant bacon?

A. You get a Porkkey.

●

Q. How does a wizard order buffalo chicken?

A. *Wingardium*!

Q. Do Slytherins drink diet soda?
A. No, they prefer Regulus.

●

Q. What sweet treats do wizards avoid?
A. Bewitched Snowballs.

●

Q. How do Slytherins warm up on a cold morning?
A. With a cup of Dracocoa.

Q. How does Voldemort like his sandwiches?

A. With the horcrux cut off.

●

Flavors We Hope Bertie Bott Never Makes

- Knut
- Unicorn Blood
- Quirrell's Unwashed Head Scarf
- Polyjuice
- Aragog Fur
- Nagini's Breath
- Inferi
- Wand
- Moaning Myrtle's Bathroom
- Skele-Gro
- Dust from the Mirror of Erised
- The Sorcerer's Stone
- Knight Bus Tire
- Mandrake
- Golden Snitch
- Boggart
- Hagrid's Tea
- Troll Boogers

Chapter 10:

IT'S MATCH DAY!

Q. What kind of cannon always misfires?

A. A Chudley Cannon.

•

Q. Why can't a quidditch player keep a secret?

A. They always snitch!

Q. Why are quidditch players bad bakers?
A. They run away from the beaters.

•

Q. What do you call two quidditch players who live in the same dorm?
A. Broom-mates.

Technically, EVERY quidditch player is a sweeper.

•

Wanting money is simply a quid-itch.

142

Q. What ball isn't good for quidditch?

A. A Yule Ball.

●

Wizards tried to train squirrels to play quidditch, but it wound up driving them nuts.

Q. Why is quidditch played on flying brooms?

A. Because it would be really hard to reach the goals if it weren't!

●

Q. What's another name for quidditch broomstick material?

A. Oliver Wood.

Q. How many Seekers does it take to change a lightbulb?

A. One, but it's worth 150 points.

•

Q. What do quidditch brooms drink?

A. Sweepy-Time Tea.

•

Q. What's the difference between baseball and quidditch?

A. One has fly balls and the other has balls that fly.

•

Q. What do wizards use instead of baby powder?

A. Quit-itch!

•

Q. When is a bell not a bell?

A. When it's Katie Bell, quidditch chaser.

144

It's Match Day!

Did you hear that the most elusive of quidditch balls ripped right through a seeker's robe? It was a case of Snitch vs. stitch.

Q. What's the difference between quidditch and Hogwarts?
A. One's played on pitches, and the other is full of witches.

•

Q. What wizards are the best at making omelets?
A. The quidditch team's beaters.

Quidditch tip: Has anybody ever tried to catch the Golden Snitch by saying, "Accio, Snitch?"

Chapter 11:

Q. Why did they call it the Shrieking Shack?

A. Because if it whispered, they would have called it the Whispering Shack.

•

Q. When did Ilvermorny open?

A. In the Ilvermorning, of course.

•

Q. What's the Crystal Cave made of?

A. Crystal.

•

Q. Why can't you go in the Forbidden Forest?

A. It's forbidden!

Q. Why didn't Moaning Myrtle flush?
A. Because it wasn't her duty.

•

Q. What do you call a negative Hermione?
A. Hermio-nay.

•

Q. What would you find on Hermione's legs?
A. Hermio-knees.

•

Q. Where do non-wizards put their coffee?
A. In their coffee muggles.

•

Q. Did you hear that Harry Potter grew a beard?
A. Now he's Hairy Potter.

•

Q. Did you hear Harry has big plans to take down Voldemort?
A. He's a regular Harry Plotter.

Jokes That Will Make You Want to Self-Obliviate

Q. Did you hear that Harry Potter gave up quidditch to play baseball?

A. He's the catcher, so now he's Harry Squatter.

•

Q. What could you also call Lily Luna Potter?

A. Potter's daughter.

•

Q. Where does Harry do all his paperwork?

A. On Potter's blotter.

•

Q. Did you hear Harry Potter bought a horse?

A. He's named him Hairy Trotter.

•

Q. What's a good name for a powerful female wizard?

A. Wanda.

Q. How do JK Tires work?

A. They rowl.

•

Q. Which side of a centaur has the most hair?

A. The outside.

•

Don't forget: Wizards who drink Polyjuice Potion are people two.

•

Q. What can you do that Harry couldn't?

A. Math. (They don't teach it at Hogwarts.)

•

Q. Why did Harry Potter get pulled over for speeding?

A. Because he didn't expect-no-patrol-man.

•

Q. Why did the Sorting Hat place Draco in Slytherin?

A. Because he was cruel and conniving.

150

Jokes That Will Make You Want to Self-Obliviate

Q. When is an owl not an owl?

A. When it's a head wig.

Q. Why does Hermione have such nice teeth?

A. Because her parents are dentists.

●

Q. How does the Invisibility Cloak work?

A. Magic!

151

Q. Why is Azkaban so horrible?

A. Because it's guarded by Dementors.

•

Q. What do most of us have in common with Draco?

A. We have a strange aunt, and he has a LeStrange aunt.

•

Q. Why do wizards and witches wear robes?

A. To stay warm!

•

Q. Who won the house ghost contest?

A. No body.

•

Q. Where do Hermione's parents live?

A. "Home, home on the grange …"

•

Q. Why are fish terrible quidditch players?

A. Because they can't fly.

Q. How does the Marauder's Map work?

A. Also magic.

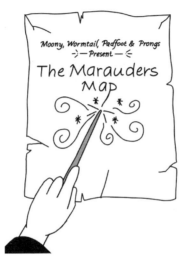

Q. Where would you find books about Beedle and Dumbledore?

A. Bards and Noble.

Q. Where does Barty Crouch sleep?

A. On his Barty couch.

Q. On what day were Harry Potter's aunt and uncle the meanest to him?

A. On Durs-day.

•

Q. What do you get when a Thestral sneezes?

A. Out of the way!

•

Q. What do you call a wizard with his hand stuck in a Thestral's mouth?

A. One-handed.

•

Q. Where does a phoenix keep all of its possessions?

A. In a Fawkes box.

•

Q. Where can you learn about what phoenixes are up to?

A. Just watch Fawkes News.

Q. What do you call an under-the-weather Dark Lord?

A. Coldemort.

•

Q. Did you hear about the Death Eater named Mark Dark?

A. Yep, Mark Dark had a dark mark.

Q. What do you call a wealthy Dark Lord?

A. Goldemort.

Q. Did you hear the Dark Lord got really into origami?

A. You can call him Foldemort.

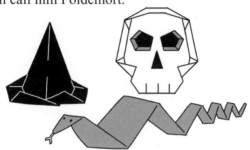

Q. Did you know that the Dark Lord was a great quidditch player?

A. Everybody called him Goaldemort.

•

Q. What happened when the Dark Lord called tech support when his wand didn't work?

A. They put him on holdemort.

•

Q. What happens when you cross the Dark Lord with old cheese?

A. Moldemort.

Q. What do you call those annoying underclassmen who adore "the boy who lived?"

A. Potter Spotters.

●

Q. What has pits and grows on a tree?

A. Cherry Potter.

●

Q. What did Draco want to do on the quidditch pitch?

A. Bury Potter.

●

Q. What do Gryffindor students have to do to keep their reputation?

A. Carry Potter.

●

Q. What do you get when you cross "the boy who lived" with a cow?

A. Dairy Potter.

Q. What do you get when you cross "the boy who lived" with a boat?

A. Ferry Potter.

●

Q. What will Ginny Weasley do one day?

A. Marry Potter.

●

Q. What's brown, digs, and is evil?

A. Moledemort.

Jokes That Will Make You Want to Self-Obliviate

Q. What's tiny, flies, and has a lightning bolt scar on its head?
A. Fairy Potter.

•

Q. How do you ask the boy who lived a question?
A. Query Potter.

•

Q. What do you get after Harry plays quidditch?
A. Wary Potter.

•

Q. What do you call Harry Potter at his most Harry Potter-ish?
A. *Very* Potter.

•

Q. What should the seventh book in the series be called?
A. *Scary Potter.*

•

Q. Did you hear that "the boy who lived" went to Nebraska?
A. They called him Prairie Potter.

Q. What do you call a part-time wizard?

A. An abracadabbler.

•

Q. Who's a real wizard of percussion?

A. Professor Drumbledore.

•

Q. What Harry Potter character has a lot of baggage?

A. Ludo Bagman.

•

Q. What's a butcher's favorite Harry Potter book?

A. *Fantastic Meats and Where to Grind Them.*

•

Q. What's a DJ's favorite Harry Potter book?

A. *Fantastic Beats and Where to Drop Them.*

•

Q. Did you hear that Jacob Kowalski wrote a book, too?

A. It's about baking and it's called *Fantastic Yeasts and Where to Bake Them.*

Q. What TV show helps little wizards learn?

A. Dumbledora the Explorer.

•

Q. Why can't great wizards play football?

A. Because they always Fumbledore.

•

Q. Where do they send the not-very-smart wizards?

A. The Dumb-strang Institute.

•

Q. Did you hear they cloned Hermione?

A. They started with Hermione, then they made Hermitwo, Hermithree . . .

•

Q. What comes after Draco?

A. Dracp, Dracq, Dracr . . .

•

Q. Why is Beauxbatons so polite?

A. They always send Fleurs.

Q. What do you get when you cross a yellow bird with "the boy who lived"?

A. Canary Potter.

Q. How does the Whomping Willow sleep at night?

A. On a Whomping Pillow.

•

Q. When Harry was at home, he had to sleep on a fold-out bed.

A. He was a cotter Potter.

•

Q. Did you hear that Finnegan had a twin?

A. He was the same-us as Seamus.

Jokes That Will Make You Want to Self-Obliviate

Q. Did you hear that Hermione took Polyjuice potion and turned into a horse?

A. Call her Hermio-neigh.

•

Q. If someone's too brave for Ravenclaw, where would they get sorted?

A. Into Bravenclaw.

•

Q. What do you call a Ravenclaw party?

A. A Ravenclaw Rave.

•

When Ravenclaws get hungry, they get powerful Cravenclaws.

•

Hagrid: You're a wizard, Harry!
Hagrid: You're a lizard, Norbert!

•

In the Harry Potter books, death is serious. Dead Sirius.

Q. What do wizards have to worry about when they get off the Knight Bus?

A. Getting muggled.

•

Q. What's a wizard's favorite folk band?

A. The Deluminators.

•

Q. Tom Riddle isn't a strange name.

A. It's just a little puzzling.

•

Q. What's type of ghost is Moaning Myrtle?

A. A pottygeist!

•

Q. Where does Harry Potter buy his furniture?

A. Pottery Barn.

•

Q. Why is the American witchcraft school the fanciest?

A. Because they have a lot of Ilver-money.

164

Jokes That Will Make You Want to Self-Obliviate

Q. Did you know the minister of magic can harness lightning?

A. He's Kingsley Shacklebolt.

●

Q. What do Hogwarts student do with their garbage?

A. They get Hagrid of it.

●

It's easy to spend all afternoon in Olivanders … just *wand*ering around.

●

Q. How do the Peverell brothers greet each other?

A. "Hallow!"

●

Q. What would Harry be without the Marauder's Map?

A. Lost!

●

Q. What else would he be?

A. In a lot of trouble!

Q. Seamus named his first three children Finn. What did he call the fourth?

A. Finn, again.

•

Q. Why can't Hogwarts students check out books in the Restricted section of the library?

A. Because they're restricted.

•

Q. How should the Knight Bus make a profit?

A. Stan at the back and Ernie the money.

•

Q. Why did Ron have to wear so many hand-me-downs?

A. Because he had lots of older brothers.

•

Q. What would you get if you gave Professor Trelawney a Time Turner?

A. Someone who knew you were going to give her a Time Turner.

Q. What can little wizards spend hours doing?

A. Filling out their *colovaria* books.

•

Q. What's an American wizard's favorite band?

A. Bon Ilvermorny.

•

Q. Did you hear about the lazy kid who wanted to go to Hogwarts?

A. He wasn't a wizard, he just wanted to wear his robe all day.

Q. Where does Hogwarts get all of its students' robes?
A. Cape Town.

•

If Harry Potter books were told from the point of view of the Dementors, it would be called *The Deathly Hellos*.

•

Q. Why are there seven horcruxes?
A. Because eight would be two many.

•

Q. How can you tell the Weasley twins apart?
A. One is named Fred, and the other is named George.

•

Q. What's black and fluffy?
A. Fluffy.

•

Q. What do Death Eaters eat?
A. Death.

Jokes That Will Make You Want to Self-Obliviate

Q. What do a kitten and Hermione have in common?
A. They both turned into a cat.

•

Ron: Hey Harry, can I borrow $10 to get something off the
 trolley on the Hogwarts Express?
Harry: Sorry, I've only got nine ... and three quarters.
We were going to tell you a really funny joke here, but somebody cast an obliviate spell at us, so what are ya gonna do?

•

**Q. Did you hear a famous rapper visited Professor
 Sprout's class?**
A. Mandrake!

•

We can't Weasley out of this with an explanation, these puns
 are Owlful.

•

Yesterday, we'll tell you this great joke about Time Turners
 ... again.

About the Author & Artist

Brian Boone is the author of the Unofficial Harry Potter Joke Book series and the Jokes for Minecrafters series from Sky Pony Press, and many other books about everything from inventions and paper airplanes to magic and music. He's written jokes for a lot of funny websites, and he lives in Oregon with his family.

Amanda Brack is the illustrator of the Creeper Diaries series and the Jokes for Minecrafters series from Sky Pony Press. She has a passion for drawing and illustration and enjoys the creativity of working on a wide variety of projects in her freelance career.